SMALL CLOUD

by Ariane

illustrated by Annie Gusman

FRANKLIN PIERCE
COLLEGE LIBRARY
RINDGE, N.H. 0346)

WALKER AND COMPANY NEW YORK

Chinaberry offers books and other
treasures for the entire family. For
a catalog, please call 1-800-776-2242.

Text copyright © 1984 by Ariane
Illustrations copyright © 1984 by Annie Gusman

Reprinted by arrangement with Dutton Children's
Books, a division of Penguin Books USA Inc.

All rights reserved. No part of this book may be
reproduced or transmitted in any form or by any
means, electronic or mechanical, including photo-
copying, recording, or by any information storage
and retrieval system, without permission in writing
from the Publisher.

First published in paperback in 1996 by Walker
Publishing Company, Inc.

Published simultaneously in Canada by Thomas
Allen & Son Canada, Limited, Markham, Ontario

Library of Congress Cataloging-in-Publication Data
Ariane.
　　Small Cloud / by Ariane ; illustrated by Annie Gusman.
　　　　p.　cm.
　　Summary: Follows the adventures of Small Cloud from its birth to
Singing River and Big Sun, through its travels across the country,
and its final evolution into rain.
　　　　ISBN 0-8027-7490-3 (pbk.)
　　　　[1. Clouds—Fiction.　2. Rain and rainfall—Fiction.
3. Hydrologic cycle—Fiction.]　I. Gusman, Annie, ill.　II. Title.
PZ7.A6866Sm　1996
[E]—dc20　　　　　　　　　　　　　　　　　　96-19046
　　　　　　　　　　　　　　　　　　　　　　　　　CIP
　　　　　　　　　　　　　　　　　　　　　　　　　AC

Printed in Hong Kong

10　9　8　7　6　5　4　3　2　1

for Lilia and Serena
and all Children of the Earth
A.

for Emilie McLeod
A.G.

In the beginning, there was Small Cloud's mother, Singing River, and her father, Big Sun.

One day Singing River called to Big Sun.
Big Sun smiled and warmed the heart of Singing River.
Singing River danced in the warmth, and a mist rose slowly into the air.

One drop at a time, Small Cloud was born.

When she was grown, she called to Singing River,
"I want to go over the mountain."
"Yes," Singing River sighed. "If Whistling Wind
will help you, and if your father, Big Sun, will
watch over you, I will wait for you."

"What lies beyond the mountain?" Small Cloud asked.
"The world," Big Sun told her.
"What is the world?" Small Cloud asked.
"Come," said Whistling Wind, "I will show you."

And he lifted Small Cloud up over the mountain
and into a valley.
"Here corn grows," Whistling Wind told her.
"Someday you may help it."
Small Cloud's shadow swooped down into
the valley and then over another mountain
to a desert.
Whistling Wind blew her across the hot earth.
"Go quickly," Big Sun urged her. "Here there is
no one to help."

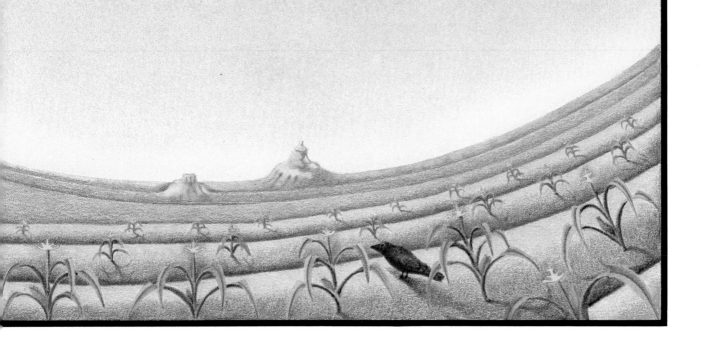

Small Cloud sped over the desert and came to a
lake where other small clouds played.
"They are just like me!" Small Cloud said.
"Go to them," said Whistling Wind. "They will
play with you."

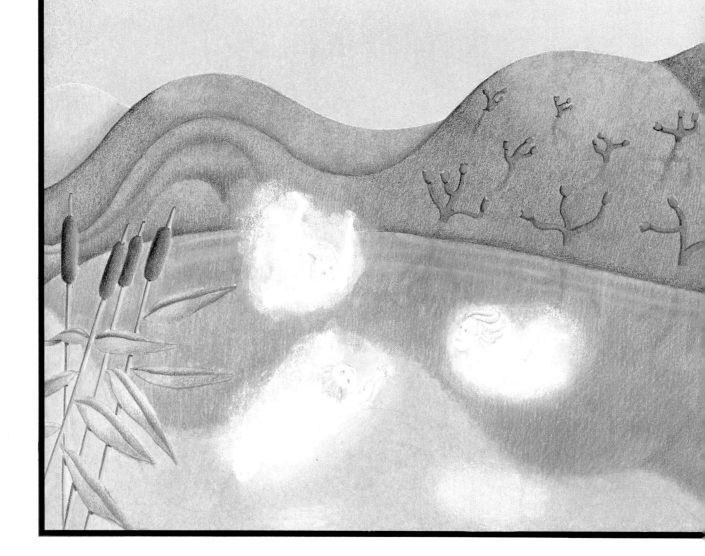

Small Cloud and her friends chased each other
above the lake.
Then, with a great gust, Whistling Wind lifted
them high over the mountains and into another
valley. "The corn is dry and the creatures are
sad," said Whistling Wind. "The earth needs rain."

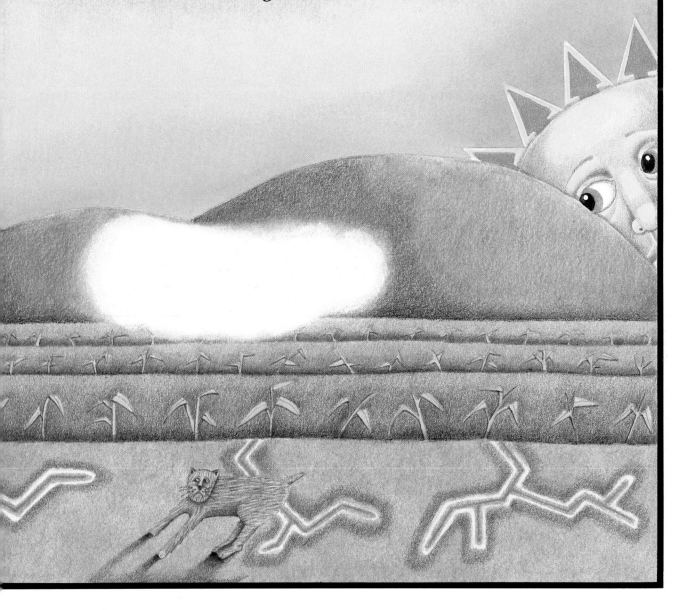

Small Cloud and her friends moved across
the sky and into each other. Together,
they became one great cloud, and rain
began to fall.
Drop by drop, Small Cloud and her friends
gave themselves to the earth.

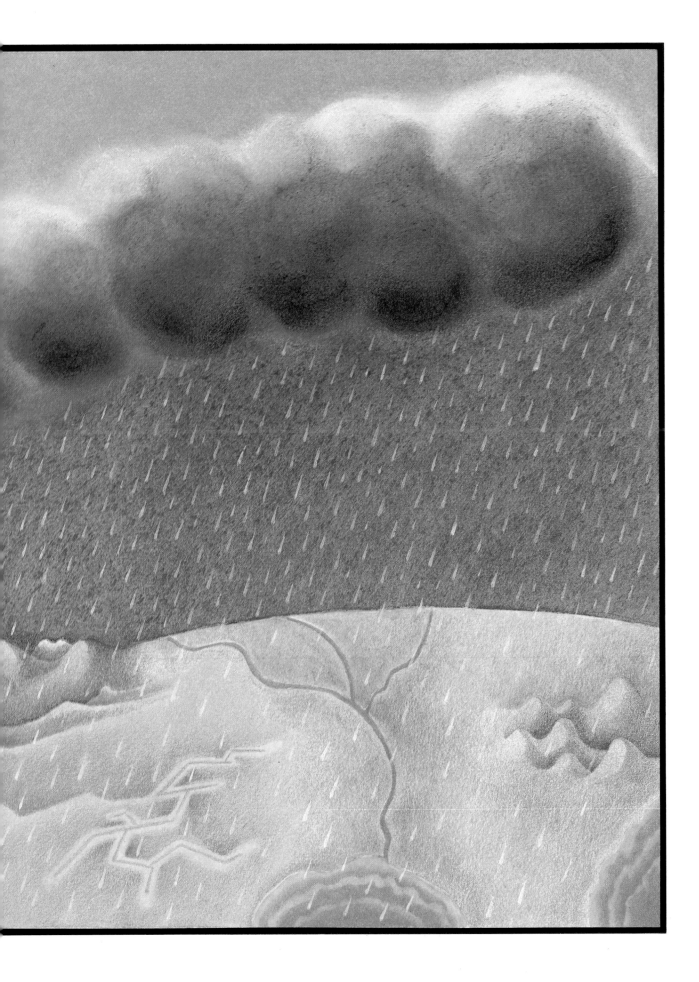

When the earth was full and the corn satisfied, Small Cloud gave her last raindrop to a river.

As Small Cloud disappeared, she heard Singing River call out, "Big Sun! Small Cloud has come home."

Big Sun smiled and warmed the heart of Singing River.

Singing River danced in the warmth, and a mist rose slowly into the air.
One drop at a time, Small Cloud was born again.